The Kidlings of Tiger Island

Quentin O. Cupp Jr.

tate publishing
CHILDREN'S DIVISION

Published by Tate Publishing & Enterprises, LLC
127 E. Trade Center Terrace | Mustang, Oklahoma 73064 USA
1.888.361.9473 | www.tatepublishing.com

Tate Publishing is committed to excellence in the publishing industry. The company reflects the philosophy established by the founders, based on Psalm 68:11,
"The Lord gave the word and great was the company of those who published it."

Book design copyright © 2012 by Tate Publishing, LLC. All rights reserved.
Cover design by Lauro Talibong
Interior design by Jake Muelle
Illustrations by JZ Sagario

Published in the United States of America

ISBN: 978-1-62024-822-5
1. Juvenile Fiction / Fantasy & Magic
2. Juvenile Fiction / Action & Adventure / General
12.09.06

Thanks to my family
for their encouragement and support.

Thanks to my daughter Stephanie
for helping me bring the Kidlings to life.

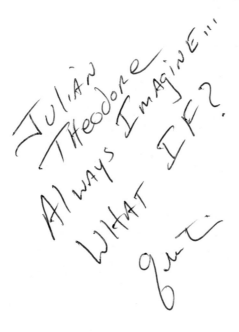

Julian
Theodore
Always Imagine"
WHAT IF?

_gw_

Chapter One

Of all the exciting, fascinating, and perilous adventures I have had in my life, the most memorable occurred in the summer of my thirteenth year. That was the summer my three sisters and I accidentally set out to sea during the worst storm of the season. By the way, my name is Danny and this is the story of the Kidlings of Tiger Island.

It all started one day when my sisters and I were sailing my dad's boat, the *Margaret K*, in a small cove near our home. The *Margaret K* was a sixteen-foot, single sail, wooden boat that my dad considered safe enough for the calm waters of the cove, but not sea worthy enough to sail out past the breakers into open waters.

Still, being confined in such a small area did not keep me from imagining myself as captain of a great sailing ship.

"All hands on deck, weigh anchor, set the main sail," I yelled out commands from the rear where I stood, bravely steering the boat with one hand on the tiller and the other hand with my forefinger pointing straight ahead. "Set a course for open water, mates."

"Will you be quiet?" snapped Lisa and Kimberly in unison. "You are so annoying."

Lisa, the older of my two older sisters now spoke alone. "How are we supposed to enjoy our sunbathing with you yelling out orders to some make believe crew? And if you have to make-believe,"—she stopped and gestured toward our younger sister who was drawing in her sketchbook— "why can't you do it quietly like Stephanie? You don't see her bothering anyone with her imagination, do you?"

"Well, quietly or not," I said, standing up and looking back toward land, "judging by how fast that storm is coming, I'd say your sunbathing is over for the day anyway."

"Yeah those are some scary looking clouds, I think you better imagine us back to shore," Kimberly said with a growing sense of urgency in her voice. "Real soon."

"Danny, watch out!" Lisa yelled, directing my attention to the fact that we were now dangerously close to the huge stones that formed the breaker walls. "Turn us around."

Suddenly all three girls were yelling. "Get us home now."

"Too late," I tried to yell over the increasing noise of the oncoming storm. "Hold on."

Crash!

The boat made a horrible sound as it hit the breaker wall, causing me to lose my footing and come down full force on the tiller.

Crack!

"Danny, get us back to shore," Lisa and Kim continued to yell.

"I can't," I answered, holding up the broken piece of tiller in my hand. "There's no way to steer the boat."

At that point we knew there was nothing we could do but watch our safe little cove disappear inside the storm that was now pushing us out into rough water, blanketed by a dark, cloudy sky.

After a long night of being tossed from wave to wave like a Ping-Pong ball, the storm began to subside long enough to allow us to lift our heads up from where we were huddled together and take a look around.

"Over there," Kimberly yelled, pointing straight ahead toward a ray of sunlight cutting through the fog. "Go toward the light, that way."

"All right, all right, let me see if I can fix this thing." I pulled my belt off and used it to lash the two broken pieces of the tiller together.

"There! Now let's see if it works." I gently moved the tiller back and forth.

"Yes!" I exclaimed. I was excited about being able to steer again. "Now let's find out where we are."

Unfortunately my newfound happiness turned quickly to disappointment as we sailed out of the fog, finding ourselves in the middle of the ocean.

"Well, Captain Waterlog," Lisa quipped sarcastically. "Did you find out where we are?"

"I'm looking, I'm looking." I answered as I looked around.

"I'm looking, I'm looking." Lisa mocked me.

"I'll tell you where we are, we're in the middle of the ocean."

"Calm down, Lisa," Kimberly spoke. "At least Danny fixed the tiller."

"Yes, he fixed the tiller, but"—Lisa paused a moment for dramatic effect before continuing her sarcastic barrage—"he wouldn't have had to fix the tiller if he hadn't broken it in the first place."

"But it was an accident." Kimberly was still trying to defend me.

"Yes, an accident that put us out here." Lisa stopped to look around. "Wherever here is."

As Kim and Lisa discussed the *what* and *why* of our situation, I happened to glance down at the picture Stephanie was sketching in her journal.

"What is that, Steph? An island?"

"Yes, Tiger Island," she answered without looking up. "It's right behind you."

"What? Where?" I turned around quickly, jerking the boat to make a hard turn, almost sending Lisa and Kim overboard.

"What are you doing?" Kim yelled at me. "I'm on your side."

"See, I told you," snapped Lisa.

"First, Captain Waterlogged gets us lost, and now he is trying to drown us!"

"Oh, yeah, look behind you!" I said triumphantly. "Captain Waterlogged has found us an island."

"But that's my Tiger Island." Stephanie quickly reclaimed the discovery of the island.

"All right, I stand corrected. It's Stephanie's Tiger Island."

"I don't care whose Tiger Island it is!" Lisa said sarcastically before acknowledging Stephanie's discovery. "Good job, little sister." Then, turning her attention back to me, her arm stretched out in the direction of Tiger Island, she sternly advised me to "get us to dry land!"

Chapter Two

As we approached the island, we noticed there wasn't any beach, only huge, jagged, black rocks that made up the shoreline and continued up the mountainside as far as we could see.

"Can you see anywhere to land?" I shouted over the noise of the wind and the waves crashing up against the rocks.

"No," replied Kim who was in front of the boat, searching for a break in the shoreline. "But I think you're going too fast toward the rocks."

"Danny!" Lisa shouted. "Look behind you, the waves are getting bigger."

I turned around just in time to get smacked in the face by one of the waves that were pushing us faster toward the island.

"Keep looking for a place to land," I shouted. "We don't have much time. Kim, what do you see?"

"Nothing but big, jagged rocks." She looked at me as if she was annoyed about having to state the obvious. "Now get us out of here."

"No, Danny!" Stephanie stood up holding onto the mast. "Go into the Tiger's mouth, over there."

I quickly turned the *Margaret K* in the direction Steph was pointing and there it was, a huge rock formation in the shape of a crouching tiger. The Tiger's eyes and nostrils were made up of four small caves cut into the mountainside directly above a much larger cave that served as the tiger's mouth. The mouth itself was lined with fang-shaped rocks that could only be seen when each wave washed back out of it into the sea.

"Hold on, everyone, we're going in," I yelled out just as a wave lifted the *Margaret K* up, up, up, and over the tiger's teeth. Up, up, up, high enough to stare into the tiger's deep, dark eyes. Up, up, up, and then down.

Crack!

The noise of the mast breaking against one of the sharp teeth could be heard over the wave that had just hurled us into to the darkness of the tiger's mouth.

Once inside, the caves turbulent current carried us quickly forward, battering the *Margaret K* against claw-shaped rock formations that reached out, ripping our sail to shreds.

Bam, bam, crunch!

The *Margaret K* was slammed from side to side against the cave walls.

"She's breaking up." I could barely hear myself over the noise of the current. "Everyone hang on."

Bam!

One more bone jarring smash against the cave wall and then silence.

"What happened?" whispered Stephanie.

"I don't know, but I think I like it," I replied as I hesitantly released the death grip I had on the side of the boat.

"The current is so calm now," Steph continued to whisper. "I just wish it wasn't so dark."

"Look up ahead," Kim spoke quietly. "I see some light; it must be the way out."

"That's not the way out." Lisa stood up for a better look. "That's a small hole in the cave wall and we're headed right for it."

"Not again," I remarked, frustrated with the entire situation. "Everyone hold on."

"Everyone hold on? Everyone hold on?" Lisa yelled back, equally as frustrated. "Is that all you can say?"

"No," I replied sarcastically. "Everyone." I paused long enough to point at the seat nearest to Lisa. "Sit down."

Bam!

The boat hit the cave wall, creating an opening large enough for us to exit the darkness of the cave into a brilliant, blinding light.

Chapter Three

I was still trying to adjust my eyes from the blinding flash when I heard Lisa and Kim commenting on our surroundings.

"Wow, it's beautiful," Lisa said in a hushed voice.

"I've never seen anything so beautiful," Kim quietly replied.

I tried to keep my voice down as well. "What do you see? What is so beautiful?"

"The colors," Stephanie replied ecstatically. "The colors of paradise."

Just then my eyes focused on a multi-colored, sandy beach, bordered by huge, multi-colored plants that seemed to be holding back the lush green forest behind them.

"Wow, it really is paradise," I agreed as I took a look around to get my bearings.

I looked down to see that we were floating in a crystal clear water lagoon inhabited by five- or six-foot long fish jumping up out of the water, changing into large birds, then back into fish as they dove back into the lagoon.

"Danny, we're floating toward the beach." Stephanie directed my attention back to the beach as she called out the colors of the sand and flowers.

"Red, yellow, blue, pink, orange…"

She was so excited that she didn't realize we had landed on the beach even before she started begging me to hurry up.

"Hurry up, Danny; I want to get off the boat. I want to get off the boat!"

"Well, if you settle down and turn around you can catch up with your sisters."

Stephanie turned around to see Lisa and Kim already on the beach, walking toward the plants at the edge of the forest.

"Hey, wait for me." She grabbed her sketchpad and colored pencils as she scampered out of the boat. "Hey, you two watch your little sister and don't go too far into the woods," I yelled as I struggled to bring the *Margaret K* ashore. "And don't worry about me, *ugh*, I've got this."

Being busy with the *Margaret K* I hadn't noticed how long the girls had been gone or that they had even returned.

"The forest is full of food." Hearing Lisa's voice caused me to turn my attention away from the *Margaret K* to where she and Kim were standing, showing off their bounty of food.

"Look," Lisa spoke "Bananas, apples, nuts…"

"Hey," I interrupted "Where is Steph?"

"Steph?" Kim echoed me "I thought she was with you."

"No! She followed you into the forest. You didn't even notice?

"Danny, she's out there all alone." Lisa's voice was full of anxiety. "We have to find her!"

"Danny, listen," Kim said. "I hear something; it sounds like crying."

"That way, Danny," Lisa said, pointing to a path into the forest. "It's coming from over there."

"You two stay here; I'll go get Steph," I said as I ran into the direction of Steph's voice. "And try not to lose each other."

By the time I reached Stephanie, it had become clear that the crying sound I thought I heard was actually Steph's giggle.

"Steph, are you okay?" I asked as I slowly approached her and noticed that she was surrounded by a dozen trees—all of which were a different color than the next. It seemed as if she was talking to the red tree directly in front her on the far side of the circle. "Who are you talking too?"

"To the trees, of course," she replied.

"To the trees?" I said sarcastically as I took her hand. "Yeah, okay. Let's see if we can find our way back to the beach."

Suddenly I was startled to hear an unfamiliar female voice behind me.

"The path to your left will take you back to the lagoon."

I turned around quickly, expecting to see someone behind me, only to find no one there.

"Who said that? Steph, did you see who said that?"

"She did," Steph replied, pointing to a figure emerging from the red tree she had been talking to.

"Who are you?" I asked, barely able to speak as I watched the figure change from bright red into a beautiful, dark-haired, suntanned girl about my own age.

"I am Kachina," she replied.

"Kachina?" I echoed. "That is a strange name?"

"It is the name given to me by my mother," Kachina explained. "In her Native American language it means *Spirit*." She paused for a second before asking me. "What do they call you?"

"I, uh, I, uh…me…I, uh." I couldn't even remember my own name as I continued to stare in amazement at Kachina.

"Don't worry about him." Stephanie tried to help me. "He's just confuzzled."

"Confuzzled?" Kachina giggled. "Now that's a strange name."

"That is not his name." Stephanie started to giggle as she began to explain.

"Confuzzled is when you are confused and puzzled at the same time."

"Danny," I blurted out. "My name is Danny, and how did you do that?" I pointed to the trees, then to Kachina, then back to the trees.

"It's what we do," Kachina answered. "We protect ourselves by blending in with our surroundings."

As she spoke, I once again stared in amazement as eleven more children of various ages emerged from the trees and joined us.

"You see," Kachina continued. "It keeps us safe until we know who we are dealing with."

"But how? How do they do that?" Once again, I pointed at the figures that seemed to be separating from the trees. "And what about those flying, swimming, fishy-birdie things back at the lagoon?"

"Confuzzled again?" Kachina asked Steph with a giggle.

"Confuzzled again." Steph laughed.

"Those flying, swimming, fishy-birdie things are called Darwins. They were named after a visitor to the island who took quite an interest in them."

Kachina continued as she began walking a path leading away from the clearing.

"Come with me to where we gather, your sisters will already be there and I can explain everything on the way."

Chapter Four

"We call ourselves Kidlings," Kachina began as we headed into the forest. "It is a name given to us by another visitor to the island because we only grow old when we choose to."

"But how?" I asked. "That's all I really want to know."

"Because of the berries that grow on the island," Kachina replied. "The berries keep us young."

"But you are not all the same age," I remarked.

"That is because not everyone begins eating the berries at the same age, and not everyone is affected the same way."

"You mean not everyone can be a tree?" I asked sarcastically.

"No, I mean that apart from becoming unseen, some of us are also Changers."

"What's a Changer?" asked Stephanie.

"A Changer is a Kidling that can alter their shape to become anything they look at," replied Kachina, pointing to the young girl walking next to Stephanie.

"Alexander is a Changer, go ahead and show her something you have sketched in your book."

"Okay, how about this?" Stephanie opened her book and began slowly flipping the pages.

Alexander took one look at the book and quickly turned from a Kidling into a dog and then back into a Kidling.

Stephanie laughed, flipped the page again, and Alexander changed into a pony.

"Pony ride, pony ride!" Stephanie shouted as she climbed on the ponies back, only to find herself laying on the ground after Alexander changed from the pony back to herself.

"Steph, Alexander, quit horsing around," I said in a joking manner before turning to Kachina. "What about those flying, swimming, fishy-birdie things? Do they eat the berries also?"

"All the animals on the island eat the berries," she replied.

"All the animals? I don't see any animals," I said, looking around.

Kachina laughed. "If you could see the animals, that would mean the berries aren't working and the animals wouldn't be protected. Take another look around." She began twirling around, arms outstretched, humming to herself.

I took another look around and this time I noticed the forest was inhabited by all kinds of crawling, walking, climbing, and flying animals.

"Wow! Those berries really work. But why didn't the Darwins become unseen to us when we were in the lagoon?"

"The Darwins have never become unseen to anyone," Kachina replied as she stopped twirling. "I wish they would become unseen; they are the most important animals on the island."

"Why are they so important?" I asked.

"The Darwins are the only animals on the island that help us harvest the berries on the first day of every twelfth full moon," Kachina explained.

"You only harvest once a year?" I said, surprised. "How do you know when it is the twelfth full moon?"

"Because," Kachina said, "we are told by Q, the keeper of the twelve; he will let us know when the Ruby Sun is placed in the twelfth hole, carved into the Stone of Time.

"Q! Who is Q?" I inquired. "And what is the Stone of Time?"

"You will find out soon," Kachina replied as she made a sweeping gesture with her arm. "We are here. The Gathering."

Chapter Five

The Gathering, as it was called, was a group of thirty or more huts constructed of saplings, bent over and held in place with large flower petals that were laced to the saplings with heavy vines.

The huts themselves were positioned in a circle around one larger hut that I guessed occupied a place of importance in the center.

As we walked into the circle toward the larger hut, I looked around for Lisa and Kim.

"Hey, I thought you said my sisters would be here?"

"They are," replied Kachina. "There, coming out of Q's hut right now."

"There they are," shouted Stephanie. "Lisa, Kim, over here."

"What are they wearing?" I snickered. "Are those giant flowers petals?"

"Yes, it is the dress of all females during each full moon celebration," Kachina answered just as Kim and Lisa reached Steph and me, throwing their arms around our necks for a group hug, then a non-stop description of their day.

"Danny, you won't believe what happened," Lisa began to tell the story only to be cut off every other sentence by Kim.

"We were waiting by the boat like you told us to."

Kim said, "All of a sudden we were surrounded by these kids—"

Lisa said, "They're called Kidlings because they never grow old—"

Kim said, "They never grow old as long as they eat berries."

Lisa said, "Magic berries that only grow on the island—"

Kim said, "Berries that they have to protect so bad guys won't become unseen—"

Lisa said, "Berries that can only be picked once a year—"

Kim said, "And Q said that the harvest might be tomorrow—"

Lisa said, "And that we can go along."

Both Lisa and Kim ended their story with a deep breath, and together they asked, "Can we go, Danny? Please!"

"Yes, we can, if only someone will tell me who this Q is that everyone keeps talking about."

"I believe they are talking about me." The voice behind me sounded too old and deep to be from a Kidling.

I turned around, startled to find a much older person standing before me.

"You're not a kid," I blurted out. "You must be at least fifty or something."

"Yes," Q responded, laughing. "I chose to grow old so I could have kids of my own." Q looked over at Kachina and then back at me. "I see you have met my youngest child, Kachina."

At that point he was joined by two husky, young boys that looked about the ages of Kim and Lisa.

"Now, I would like you to meet my two sons, Moon and Stars."

I remember at that point thinking how sickeningly sweet Lisa and Kim sounded as they swooned.

"And who doesn't love the moon and stars?"

After introducing Moon and Stars, Q announced that it was time to go to the Stone of Time. He then turned to face a large rectangle stone, three feet high, two feet long, and a foot wide, with twelve deep holes carved out along the top. Q reached his hand into the eleventh hole and pulled out a large red ruby and held it high for us all to see.

"This is the symbol of our full moon, the moon that gives us long life."

He then lowered the ruby, depositing it into the twelfth hole of the Stone of Time.

"Tonight we rest." His voice boomed over the crowd that had assembled around him. "For tomorrow, the Darwins will lead us to the harvest."

Chapter Six

Long before the next morning sunrise, we had already journeyed far into the forest, which was well lit by the brilliance of the full moon. Kachina and I were at the front of the caravan, followed closely by Stephanie and Alexander, who were followed not so closely by Lisa, Kim, Moon, and Stars.

The rest of our little parade consisted of the entire Kidling population, except for a chosen few who had remained at the Gathering with Q.

"Kachina, why are the Darwins flying ahead of us?" I asked. "Are we following them?"

"Yes, they will lead us to the berry trees."

"You mean we don't know where we are going?" I asked, surprised.

"We are going to pick berries," Kachina answered, sounding a bit irritated. "But we don't want any visitors to know the whereabouts of the berry trees so we never mark the way."

Just then Lisa shouted. "Look, the Darwins are landing on that hilltop. Does that mean we are there?"

"No, it just means we will be out of the forest soon and into the foothills," Moon answered. "We will rest here until the Darwins fly again."

As we gathered at the base of the foothill, several of the younger Kidlings formed a circle around Kachina. "Tell us more about the travels of Q!" they begged her.

"Yeah, I'd like to hear some stories as well," I spoke up. "You did promise yesterday that you would tell me more about him."

"All right." Kachina smiled. "Just one story while we rest."

Chapter Seven

Travels of Q

"Q is a Traveler," Kachina began. "A Traveler is a Kidling that is sent to the outside world to gain knowledge and gather news of current events to bring back to the island."

One of the younger Kidlings interrupted. "Also, because of powers he can only use off the island, he is able to help others in the outside world."

"Yes," Kachina agreed. "Travelers have helped out in many ways. Like the time Q tied that key to Ben Franklin's kite, that was a real shocker."

"Or the time he switched treasure maps with Blackbeard the pirate." Moon laughed. "Q returned the treasure chest to its rightful owners and Blackbeard was left with a treasure chest full of rotten apples."

"Yeah, and if he hadn't kept pinching that Michelangelo guy, he never would have finished that painting on the ceiling."

"But not all Travelers have had as much fun as Q, and not all Travelers have returned from the outside world," Kachina said sadly.

"But Q has returned many times and my favorite story is about the time he returned with a Native American woman named Shadow." Kachina's eyes sparkled and seemed to glow as she began to tell the story.

"Q was eighteen years old, an age he had been for many years, when one of his travels put him somewhere in your America. The year was 1861 and the United States was in the middle of a civil war that he knew nothing about. He did know enough to hide behind some fallen trees when the roar of the cannons and muskets became louder and louder, until the air around him started exploding with the *crack, crack, crack* of the musket balls ripping through the brush and tree limbs.

As he lay there watching the battle rage on, a Yankee soldier knelt down next to him and fired a shot. Then, looking down at Q's clothing and slightly darker skin, he mistook him for a runaway slave."

"Don't worry, son, you're safe now. Come with me."

"The next couple of months, Q lived and worked with other runaway slaves, performing duties for the Union officers. His favorite duty was hunting for food in the forest because it gave him the chance to help runaway slaves on their journey north.

One day, shortly after the Union troops had marched into a hilly, woody area of South Carolina, Q was dispatched into the woods to search for food. As he leaned, unseen, up against a tree, a young, Native American girl around his age walked by, stepping on his foot."

"Ouch!" Q tried to muffle his voice so he wouldn't startle the girl.

"Who are you? Where did you come from?" the girl asked, turning quickly, and surprised to see Q standing next to the tree she had just passed.

"I am Q. I was standing behind the tree when you passed by."

"You are wearing the clothes of a Union soldier." The girl was frightened and turned to run.

"No. Don't go. I won't hurt you." Q reached out and took hold of the girl's hand. "I'm not a soldier. I only hunt and cook for the officers. They think I am a runaway slave."

"But you are not a slave?" the girl asked.

"No," replied Q. "But what about you? You remind me of a tribe of people I once lived with on another travel."

Q paused for a moment to take a look at the girl.

"You are not of the white man's world. What do they call you?"

"In your language, my name is Shadow. It was given to me by my mother because I followed her wherever she went."

"Where is she now?"

"My mother and I were given to the master of a plantation to pay off a debt owed to him by our chief."

"What about your father?"

"My father was a brave warrior who died for his people," Shadow answered proudly. "He waits for my mother and me with all and everything in the great beyond."

Suddenly, the pride in her voice turned to fear as the quiet of the forest was shattered by musket fire and screams coming from just over the hill in front of them.

"My mother!" she cried, pointing in the direction of the gunfire. "That's the plantation where we live!"

By the time Q and Shadow reached the hilltop, the skirmish between the Union and the rebel troops was over. The Union troops were setting fire to the main house and surrounding buildings and it was evident that no one from the plantation had survived the attack.

"Mama!" whispered Shadow, dropping to her knees, crying.

Q knelt down next to her, gently wrapping his arms around her shoulders.

"There is nothing here for you anymore, Shadow, and it is time for me to leave. Come home with me."

Kachina paused for a moment and then smiled. "And that is the story of how my mother came to live here on Tiger Island."

"One more, one more," the younger Kidlings pleaded. "Tell us one more!"

"I only promised you one." Kachina laughed. "Besides, it is time to go," she said, pointing to the sky. "The Darwins are flying again."

As we continued our journey out of the woods and across the foothills, Kachina explained to me that Q had quit eating berries because he wanted to grow old with her mother, Shadow.

"Where is your mother now?" I asked.

"Several years ago she became part of all and everything," Kachina replied.

"All and everything?" I questioned.

"Yes, all and everything around us," Kachina said, stretching her arms out above her head.

"Look," Lisa called out, "the Darwins are landing. Does that mean they want to rest again?"

"Not this time." Moon smiled. "Listen to all the noise they are making. They are telling us that the berries are on the other side of that hill." Moon paused to scan the sky behind him. Then, he grabbed Lisa's hand and began running up the hill. "And we want to be on that hilltop before the sun cast its light down on the trees."

"To the top of the hill!" Stars shouted out as he began his charge up the hill with Kim in tow.

"We have to hurry if we want to see the trees come to life."

"I want to see the trees come to life," I said, grabbing Kachina by the hand and joining in the race.

"Come on, Steph, Alexander, to the top."

As we reached the hilltop we could see a shallow valley between the foothill and the mountainside. In the valley there were rows of trees that were completely bare—no leaves, no flowers, no berries, nothing.

"Are we in the right place?" I asked as I searched the tree limbs for any sign of vegetation. "Are you sure the Darwins know where the berries are?"

"*Sh.*" Kachina pressed her forefinger against my lips.

"Here comes the sun."

The sunlight slowly made its way through the forest, up the foothills, then down into the valley of trees.

"Watch," whispered Stars. "The berries can only be seen in the light of day."

The anticipation of what was about to happen seemed to take on a life of its own, drawing us close together, hand in hand, until we were barely breathing.

Suddenly, as if a blanket was being pulled off the rows of trees, the sunlight lit up their branches, bringing them to life with an abundance of multi-colored berries growing right before our eyes.

"It's amazing," exclaimed Lisa and Kim. "Amazing and beautiful. Just look at all the colors."

"That is a lot of berries," I remarked, staring in awe at the now bountiful trees. "Are we going to pick all of those berries?"

"Yes, so we better get started," Kachina answered as she ran down the hill toward the berry trees. "Just watch out for Coco."

The next question I asked as I followed her down the hill—"What is a Coco?"—was answered by a loud fierce yell.

Rah!

Instantly, I was lying on my back, looking up at a six-foot, orange, furry monster with razor-sharp teeth and fiery red eyes. *Rah,* the monster roared again as I attempted to crawl backward up the hill, all the while trying to keep an eye on the monster who was now rearing back to let out one more ferocious roar. I was surprised when the monster finally lowered his head to within inches of mine and softly said, *meow.*

I lay on my back for a few more seconds, scared and puzzled, until I heard Moon and Stars laughing.

"What are you two laughing about?" I yelled screamed. "What is so funny?"

"You are," Moon answered before Stars cut him off.

"Are you afraid of our little Coco?" Stars asked sarcastically.

"Little Coco?" I yelled again. "Did you see the size of that monster? It's gigantic?"

Moon and Stars continued laughing, pointing toward the monster. "Look, the big, bad monster is gone now," said Moon.

"Yeah, I think you scared it to pieces," Stars agreed.

"What do you mean?" I turned around, expecting to be face to face, once again, with the monster.

Instead, I found myself looking down at dozens of brightly colored, grapefruit-size, fuzzy balls…with eyes?

Kachina walked over and stood in the middle of the small creatures.

"These cute little bundles of fur are called Cook-Cooks. They are here to protect the berry trees from any outsiders," Kachina explained as she bent down, scooping up the orange one nearest her.

"And this one is their leader, Coco. I believe you two have met."

As she placed Coco in my hands, it looked up at me innocently, and, half-smiling, let out a soft whispered, *Rah*.

"Very funny, very funny," I repeated over and over to everyone mimicking Coco's, *Rah,* as they passed me on their way to the berry trees.

"Very funny, very funny."

Chapter Eight

We spent the rest of the morning filling pillow case-sized, hollow plant leaves with the berries we picked from the lower branches of the trees. Whenever we had two of the hollow plant leaves full, we would tie the open ends together, creating saddlebags that could be placed on the back of a Darwin and flown back to the Gathering.

"Well, now that we have picked all the berries from the lower branches," I said, looking up and pointing to the treetops, "how do we get the berries way up there?"

"That's the fun part," replied Kachina as she picked up a Cook-Cook, gently tossing it up into a nearby berry tree. "The Cook-Cooks really enjoy this game."

I looked up to watch the Cook-Cook bounce from limb to limb, causing the berries to shake loose and rain down on us.

"Bouncy, bouncy, bouncy," Stephanie playfully sung the words, referring to the action of the Cook-Cook in the tree.

"Bouncy, bouncy, bouncy."

Within minutes, Stephanie's playful tune was being repeated by a chorus of Cook-Cooks that had gathered at her feet.

"Bouncy, bouncy, bouncy. Bouncy, bouncy, bouncy," they continued to sing happily as we tossed them high into the trees, causing a shower of berries.

"This is more like it," I remarked as we returned to the chore of filling hollow plant leaves.

"Yes, every chore should be this fun," commented Lisa as she joined Kim who was watching Moon and Stars gather berries.

"You're right, Lisa," whispered Kim. "It's almost like not working at all."

As I looked around I could see that Lisa and Kim were not the only ones more interested in something other than picking berries.

Stephanie and Alexander had gathered some of the younger Kidlings under a berry tree and were busy putting on a show for them. As Stephanie flipped through the drawing of animals in her sketchbook, Alexander would take on the various forms as the younger Kidlings yelled out the animals names.

"Cat. Bird. Fish out of water." They laughed and giggled.

"Lion. Tiger. Bear."

"Oh my," Alexander said exhausted. "Slow down, I am getting dizzy."

"You're not dizzy yet," Stephanie said, sketching a spinning top, which she flashed in front of Alexander. "Now you're really going to be dizzy."

Stephanie quickly wrapped a vine around Alexander, who was now in the shape of a giant top and gave it a yank. The younger Kidlings laughed and playfully yelled for help as they ran off in all directions to avoid the giant spinning top.

Chapter Nine

I was enjoying watching everyone have fun so much that it took me a few minutes to realize that Kachina had stopped picking berries and was standing stone-still, staring at the sky, back toward the forest.

"What's wrong, Kachina?"

"*Shh*, be quiet, Danny, listen."

"Listen to what? I don't hear a thing."

It was then that I noticed that no one or anything—not the Darwins, not the Kidlings, not even the Cook-Cooks were making a sound—the entire island had fallen eerily quiet.

"Up there!" shouted Moon, who was pointing at a Darwin that was having trouble flying toward us.

Squawk, the Darwin cried out in pain, desperately flapping its one good wing in order to maintain flight.

Squawk. The shrill, bone chilling sound seemed to echo over the entire island.

"Stars, what's wrong with the Darwin?" Kim asked. "Why is it flying like that?"

"It looks like a broken wing," Stars answered.

"No, it has been shot," shouted Moon.

"Shot?" Lisa, Kim, and I repeated the word loudly, almost in shock.

"Yes, shot," declared Moon, just as the Darwin landed at his feet and immediately collapsed.

"Is that an arrow?" I asked as Moon pulled it from the Darwin's wing.

"Who shoots a Darwin? And why use a bow and arrow?" I wondered out loud.

"Because a bow and arrow does not make any noise," Kachina answered as she knelt down next to the Darwin and began stroking its head. "He doesn't want us to know that he is here."

"Who is he that doesn't want us to know that he is here?"

"X," answered Kachina, with a bit of hesitation in her voice. "X is here."

Within seconds we were surrounded by Kidlings passing on the news in hushed voices.

"X is here. Pass it on."

"X! Not another letter," I said sarcastically. "Who named you people, the alphabet fairy?"

Kachina's immediate reaction was anger as she blurted out, "It is not funny. X is the descendent of a Kidling who was banished from the island by Q many twelve moons ago." She continued to sooth the wounded Darwin as she explained.

"X's ancestor Ramos was kicked off the island for helping some outsiders attempt to steal our berries."

"When Q caught him, he branded Ramos on the forehead with the letter X and told him from now until the last twelfth moon, you and your descendents will carry this mark and be banished from the island."

Stephanie quit drawing in her book long enough to ask, "What happened next? Did Ramos leave the island?"

"Yes," Kachina continued. "But not before he jumped up and grabbed Q's dagger and swore he would return to the island, and"—Kachina paused and raised her hand up over her head as if she were holding a knife—"with your very own dagger I will take my revenge on you and all Kidlings."

"Did he ever return?" asked Stephanie.

"No," replied Kachina. "Ramos left the island, never to return. But his descendents have returned on many twelfth moons, attempting to fulfill his vow of revenge. "This last descendent has been the meanest yet."

"Does this look like him?" Stephanie asked, holding up a sketch of a very dark, menacing figure, his face full of anger was made even more frightening by the large letter "X" scarred into his forehead.

"Yes," Kachina hissed, her eyes full of contempt. "That's him. That's X."

She quickly turned away, directing her attention to the wounded Darwin that had now begun to glow brightly.

"What's happening?" I whispered.

"It is time to go now." Kachina raised her arms above her head, her hands stretched out toward the sky, just as the Darwin became hundreds of tiny, iridescent lights floating in a swirling motion up into the trees.

"Take your place with all and everything."

It was Moon's voice that brought our attention back to the fact that X was on the island.

"Kachina, come on. Q is in danger; we must get back to the Gathering."

Chapter Ten

I turned around just in time to watch Moon and the other Kidlings straddle the backs of Darwins that were now hovering several feet above the ground.

Turning back I saw Kachina was sitting on the back of one Darwin, while motioning to me to climb up on the back of another Darwin next to her. "Hurry, we have to leave now. Just jump up and hold on."

I looked around quickly to check on Stephanie and her sisters, but I could not find them. "What about the girls, where are they?"

"Don't worry, they are already on their way with Moon and Stars," Kachina shouted back, sounding more urgent than before. "Hurry please, we must leave now!"

In a matter of seconds the Darwins were skimming the treetops as we held on, trying, unsuccessfully, to dodge the branches that seemed to be reaching out in an attempt to knock us off.

"Can't we fly any higher?" I raised my head just in time to receive a mouthful of leaves.

"No," shouted Kachina as she guided her Darwin closer to me. "We are too heavy for the Darwins to fly any higher. Just keep your head down and your mouth shut."

I put my head down and continued to fight off the tree branches when I heard Moon shout.

"Kachina, we are not going toward the Gathering, we are going to the lagoon."

He had lifted his head up for a brief moment to get his bearings. "Q must have gone to the lagoon to keep X from entering the forest."

"There they are," shouted Stars. "Down there by the waters edge of the lagoon."

I looked down to see that a dozen, well-armed men had formed a circle around the half-dozen Kidlings that had remained with Q back at the Gathering.

"Where's Q?" I shouted. "I don't see him anywhere."

"This way, he's over here," answered Stars as he guided his Darwin down toward two figures struggling near the edge of the forest. The larger figure was dressed entirely in black from his boots to his beret, which he wore turned round backward so as not to hide the large letter "X" scarred into his forehead. The smaller figure was Q and he was bleeding from several wounds inflicted by X—wounds that left Q with only one good arm to fight with, and that was the arm X had pinned in between the two of them as he began yelling, "You banished my family from this island and cursed us with mortality." He yelled as he cut a letter "X" into Q's chest. "Now it is my turn to banish you from this island by claiming revenge for my ancestors."

X thrust the dagger into the center of the letter "X" he had just carved into Q's chest.

"*Ah*," Q screamed as he fell to his knees clutching the dagger.

"No," Kachina cried out as she jumped down from her Darwin. "Get away from him." She pushed X out of the way and knelt down next to Q wrapping her hands around his hands on the dagger. "Moon, help me get this dagger out."

Tears were now streaming down her face as she pleaded for help. "Stars, bring me some berries so I can treat him."

"No, Kachina," Q spoke softly. "It is time for me to go now."

"But we can save you. Moon, Stars, tell Q we can make him better," Kachina pleaded as she wiped away her tears.

"No," Q insisted, holding his right hand up toward Moon and Stars. "Take my hand, my sons, and promise me from this day on you will protect the harvest of this island and all who live here."

"I promise," Moon said quietly as he knelt next to Q.

Stars, however, let go of Q's hand as he shouted, jumping toward X.

"I'll make you pay for this, you'll never leave this island alive."

"No, Stars," Q moaned in pain as he tried to sit up. "You must promise." He paused to catch his breath while looking around at Moon and Kachina. "You all must promise never to allow a Kidling to seek revenge in my name. Now promise."

Kachina, her voice quivering, tried to fight back the tears. "We promise, Daddy. We all promise, but please let us help you."

Q looked up at her and smiled. "Please don't cry for me, my Kachina. I have seen the twelfth moon hundredths of times and I am tired." Then, just before closing his eyes, Q looked at his three children. "I am ready to join your mother. I am ready to become part of all and everything."

Kachina leaned over kissing Q's forehead tenderly, just as his body separated into hundredths of tiny lights that swirled away up into the trees.

I leaned down to comfort Kachina, but I was pushed away by Stars who grabbed the dagger from her hand and spun around pointing it at X. "Q is gone because of you, so now it is time for you to take your place with all and everything."

"I don't think so." X laughed. "Remember your promise. No Kidling is allowed to seek revenge in the name of Q."

I can't remember exactly what happened next, but suddenly I was standing next to Stars with Q's dagger in my hand bravely announcing. "Well, I am not a Kidling, so I guess you will have to deal with me."

X took one look at me and started to laugh. "You want to fight me man to man? Come on then, show me what you've got." X pulled his dagger from its sheath, swinging it wildly from side to side while walking toward me. I quickly took several steps back until I was standing knee deep in the lagoon.

"Look at you." X laughed even louder. "You're all wet and I'm getting bored." With that, X lunged toward me, plunging his dagger deep into my chest.

I could hear my scream echo off the mountainside, sending an anguished sound into the forest. I screamed once more as he pulled his dagger from my chest, letting my body fall into the lagoon, still clutching Q's dagger in my right hand.

"Danny, Danny," Kachina 's voice replaced the sound of my own that was now echoing through the forest as I sank deeper into the cool water of the lagoon, watching the surface getting farther and farther away until everything was a blur.

Then a streak of color flashed before my eyes, followed by another then another—it was the Darwins. They were swimming around me, creating thousands of air bubbles, joining together to form a large air pocket, allowing me to breath as I continued to sink to the bottom of the lagoon.

"Danny, I'm coming to get you," I heard Kachina call out, but this time it sounded as if it was a thought put inside my head by someone else, or maybe I was dreaming. "I'm coming to get you."

I was sure I was dreaming now because off in the distance I could see a translucent shape swimming toward me. "Kachina, is that you?" I tried to focus on the figure getting closer. "It is you, but how?" I spoke softly, not knowing if she could hear me.

When she reached the bottom of the lagoon where I was resting, she slid one hand inside my air bubble, gently placing it on my forehead. Immediately we could hear each other's thoughts.

"Danny, I'm so glad the Darwins helped you. I couldn't stand to lose you, too."

I could tell her thoughts were more revealing than she had intended them to be, causing her to quickly finish her thought. "Besides, you have to finish what you started."

My own thoughts came slowly. "I'm hurt and I can't move. I don't think I can fight."

"But you must fight, Danny, and you must win."

She slipped her other hand into my air bubble and placed it over the wound in my chest. "From this day on, through the magic of the berries, our hearts and minds will be joined, giving you the ability to fight with the power and strength of many."

Pow! The air bubble around me exploded.

I frantically reached out for Kachina, wrapping my arms around her.

"I'm going to drown."

"You're all right." She tried to calm me down. "You can breathe down here just as well as you can up there." She pointed up toward the surface.

"Up there, we have to get up there." I let go of Kachina and started swimming. "We can't let X leave the island with the berries."

"Grab hold of a couple of Darwins—they will get us to the surface faster."

I grabbed the first pair of Darwins swimming near by, hoping they could understand me.

"Take me to the surface."

Whoosh. They took off as I glanced around, making sure Kachina was behind me.

"I'm right behind you." She shot me a thought as we continued to pick up speed.

Faster and faster until we burst out of the lagoon in a spray of water twenty to thirty feet high, Kachina and I were still holding onto our separate pair of Darwins that were halfway through their transition from fish to birds, and Kachina was still partially translucent. I am sure we must have resembled some sort of creatures right out of a mid-evil fountain.

Chapter Eleven

The first voice I heard as I landed on the beach was Stephanie's. "Danny you're alive," she cried out joyously.

The second voice came from an astonished X. "Alive! You can't be alive. I sent you to the bottom of the lagoon."

"Yes, you did, but I am back, stronger then ever." I thrust my dagger high in the air, striking a pose like some mighty returning warrior.

Kachina leaned toward me, whispering in my ear, "You have to talk out loud now, Danny. X can't hear your thoughts the way I can."

"Oh, no wonder he is looking at me kind of confuzzled."

"Well, you do look silly just standing there like a statue."

"All right, all right, let me try again. This time I will use my big boy voice."

I looked straight into X's eyes and repeated, "Yes, you did, but I am back better than ever."

"That was much better, Danny." Kachina was once again whispering in my ear.

"I am so glad I could make you happy." I gave her a fake grin before turning back toward X. "Now, how about we finish this little matter of kicking your butt off my island."

Hearing me refer to Tiger Island as my island caused X to laugh. "Since when did this become your island?"

"The moment he was willing to fight and die for it" Kachina replied to X, "that was the moment he became one of us." She paused for a moment before announcing, "That makes him a Kidling, which makes this his island."

I was so focused on what Kachina was saying that I didn't notice X had been slowing moving toward Stephanie.

"So you're a Kidling now." X became very animated, turning in circles, waving his arms around, moving closer to Stephanie. "So I guess that is your tree and that is your lagoon and you alone are going to go against Q's last request by seeking revenge in his name."

"I am not seeking revenge against you. I am protecting what is ours."

Suddenly Moon placed his hand on my left shoulder. "He won't have to do it alone. Will he, Stars?" Moon asked as Stars joined us, placing his hand on my other shoulder before declaring. "As long as he is a Kidling, he will never be alone."

I let out a huge sigh of relief, then I bravely spoke up. "All right, let's kick the X out of this guy."

X was now standing directly behind Stephanie. "Not so fast, everybody freeze." He yelled as he grabbed her. Everybody, including his own men, stood perfectly still.

"Not you guys," He yelled, clearly aggravated. "You guys grab those sacks from those overgrown feather dusters." He pointed at several Darwins still carrying their load of berries. The men began walking slowly toward the Darwins as the lead man, the one called Whip, tried to coax them into standing still. "We're not going to hurt you birdies, we just want to help you get those heavy sacks off your backs."

"Fly away, Darwins, fly away," Kachina shouted. "Fly away."

Several of the Darwins took off immediately while others jumped into the lagoon, quickly swimming away, leaving Whip and the other men running around in circles.

Whip untied the bullwhip he always carried on his side and started swinging it around over his head. "I'll get at least one of you," he shouted. Crack went the bullwhip again and again with no results until, *crack!* The whip came down hard on one of the Darwins still running around on the beach. "I got one over here men, help me grab the berries." Whip hollered as he and the rest of the men ran toward the wounded Darwin. Just before reaching the Darwin, the men were sent reeling back on their heels by a loud, ferocious roar—"*Rah.*" The fiery orange monster came bounding out of the forest sending Whip and the other men racing back to their boat in the lagoon, pulling and pushing each other along the way.

"Coco, I sure am glad to see you." I laughed, watching the men fight to get aboard their boat.

"It doesn't matter what my men do, Danny," X reminded me. "Did you forget I have your sister?"

"No, I didn't forget," I answered, feeling more confident about the outcome of our situation. "Stephanie, show Alexander your sketch book."

Stephanie started flipping the pages of her book until she found one she liked. She flashed it in front of Alexander, who changed her shape and roared. "Meow."

"Is that a cat? Are you really a cat?" Stephanie asked surprised, tapping on the book. "The other page Alexander, look at the other page."

Alexander looked again. "*Roar.*"

"A lion," X screamed as he fell backward, releasing his grip on Stephanie.

"Run, Steph, run," I shouted as she took off into the woods with Alexander.

Several of X's men had left the boat and were helping him up from where he had been cowering from the lion.

"Don't worry about me," X hollered. "Go get that girl."

As the men followed Stephanie into the woods I began shouting out orders.

"Coco, take some Cook-cooks to help Stephanie."

"Some of you Kidlings go with them."

"Moon, Stars, bring X over to me."

Moon and Stars grabbed X by his arms and dragged him to where I was standing.

I reached down, taking his dagger from its sheath. "You better hope your men don't hurt my sister, or when I get back this dagger will rest forever in your heart."

Chapter Twelve

I had only gotten several hundred feet into the woods when I noticed three of X's men standing in a clearing looking completely confused and puzzled.

"Confuzzled," I whispered to myself with a slight grin. "I think I'll stay around and watch the show."

From my vantage point I heard them decide to split up and take different paths further into the woods.

The man that took the path to the left of the clearing had just turned a corner in the path when he came face to face with about twenty Cook-cooks.

"Bouncy-bouncy, bouncy-bouncy," they purred as they surrounded the man.

"What do we have here? You want to go bouncy-bouncy?" The man started tossing the Cook-cooks in the air, only to let them fall to the ground instead of catching them. "Now, if you don't take me to the girl I'm going to stomp you into the ground." His voice became angry. "Bouncy-bouncy will become stomp-stomp. You hear me? Stomp-stomp."

Suddenly the ground began to shake and the sky grew very dark. The man slowly looked up, finding himself in the shadow of a fiery orange beast, its eyes full of anger and its mouth full of razor-sharp teeth glistening every time it spoke. "Stomp, stomp."

The monster moved forward, flashing a sly, menacing smile. "Stomp-stomp."

The man started slowly backing away from the monster when he tripped over a Cook-cook, landing him face down in the middle of the group of Cook-cooks he was going to stomp on. Each one of them were flashing razor-sharp teeth and speaking in deep, eerie voices. "Stomp-stomp, Stomp-stomp."

The man screamed, jumped up, and ran down the path, crashing headfirst into the second man who was stumbling into the clearing muttering something about big mean trees.

It seems the second man spotted a couple of Kidlings running down the path ahead of him.

"Stop right there," he yelled, picking up a large, club-shaped tree limb. "I see you, you can't hide from me." He walked down the path smacking every other tree with the club. "Which tree did you fade into? Was it this one or this one?" Smack went the club. "Wrong again, okay, how about this one?" The man continued to club each tree until… *swoosh, slap.*

The tree's branches began to slap the man on his arms, legs, head, and one strong slap on his back that sent him somersaulting over a log in the path.

The man stood up quickly and began yelling and clubbing the tree nearest to him. "I know you're in there. Take that and that and…"

Just then a Kidling appeared out of a tree limb overhead and snatched the club out of the man's hand.

It sounded as if he were singing as he repeatedly bonked the man on the head.

"And that and that and that."

The man finally stumbled away and headed down the path to the clearing and his unfortunate accident with the first man.

Now, as much fun as it was watching the first and second man's misadventure, I believe watching the third man's ordeal was the best.

It seemed the third man had chosen the same path as Steph and Alexander. As I watched him, he began walking very slowly and hunched over as if he were sneaking up on someone.

I looked ahead down the path and could see Stephanie; she was standing in the middle of the path with her back toward the man. I jumped up to warn her, but before I could call out, the man grabbed her from behind.

"I got you," he yelled excitedly, obviously pleased with the fact that he was the one to capture Steph.

"I got you and now you're coming with me."

Just then a voice from behind the man announced. "I don't think so."

The man jerked his head around to see another Stephanie hiding in the bushes nearby.

"Who? What? How?" He jerked his head back and forth from one Stephanie to the other.

"Kind of confuzzling, Isn't it?" both Stephanies remarked, giggling.

"Now look at this," said the Stephanie hiding in the bushes, opening her sketchbook to show the man.

"Is that what I think it is?" gulped the man, still holding the fake Stephanie.

"Yes, it is," said the real Stephanie, giggling out loud. "Half porcupine, half bear." She paused for a second, as if making up the name on the spot. "It's a Porcu-Bear. Do you still want to hold on?"

Before the man could answer, Alexander changed into the Porcu-Bear, turned around, and shot the man in the foot with a long, pointed porcupine needle, sending him hopping down the path screaming in pain.

"Ouch!" I said out loud to myself. "That sounds like it hurts."

"Yeah, it's definitely going to leave a mark." One of the several Kidlings who had just walked up behind me laughed.

"How about it, Danny? Let's say we get Stephanie and Alexander and head back to the lagoon."

"Yeah, let's say we do that."

Chapter Thirteen

As the Kidlings and I followed Steph and Alexander out of the woods onto the beach by the lagoon, we heard laughter coming from the direction of X's boat.

"Hey, what's so funny?" I asked, quickly stepping out of Lisa and Kim's way as they rushed by me to check on their little sister.

"Go ahead. You tell him Stars." Moon busted out laughing.

"Well, Danny, we've got every one of X's men tied to their oars, except for this guy." Stars was standing next to an unfortunate man with a large, sharp needle protruding from his foot.

"All right then, just tie him to the tiller. He can steer the boat while the others row." I walked around on the beach to where I could see X, chest deep in water, tied to the front of the boat.

Upon seeing me, he became very aggravated. "Don't think I'm done with you, I'll be back and then...*blub, blub, blub.*" X momentarily disappeared beneath a rush of water as the boat bobbed up and down in the lagoon.

Upon resurfacing, X was coughing, spitting, and still yelling out threats until Moon interrupted him.

"If I we're you I would be less concerned about us and more concerned about learning to hold your breath for long periods of time."

Splash! X disappeared again beneath another rush of water.

As we gathered together to watch X's boat glide across the lagoon and into a cave that would take them to the open sea and home, I was suddenly overcome with a strange feeling of delight and sadness.

"Hey, Danny. Why so sad looking?" Stars asked. "You're not going to miss those guys are you?"

"Not one little bit," I answered, trying to hide my feelings.

"Then what's the matter?" Kachina asked.

"I'm not sure; I think it would be great to stay on this island forever, but…"

"But you really want to get back home," Kachina finished my thought for me.

"I think it would be great to get back home, but I guess that really doesn't matter," I said, looking off in the direction of X's boat. "Since the only seaworthy boat on the island is now headed for open seas."

"What about that boat?" Kachina grabbed my shoulders, turning me toward a boat sailing out of a cove off the lagoon.

"The *Margaret K*!" I yelled. I was surprised as I watched the boat sail out of the cove into the clear, cool water of the lagoon. "She looks brand new."

"Come on, Danny!" yelled Moon as he manned the tiller, steering the *Margaret K* toward the beach. "We live on an island. Don't you think we know a few things about fixing boats?"

"Yeah," Stars spoke up with pride in his voice. "Just ask that Chris Columbus guy. We fixed him up so he could go on to discover the New World."

Moon looked at Stars and rolled his eyes. "Of course, it was the same New World that the Native Americans discovered years earlier." He jumped from the boat onto the beach and tied the bowline to a nearby tree stump.

"Now let's get you guys back to the New World."

I looked around, confuzzled. "Back to the New Wor...I mean home. But how? I don't even have any maps; I can't even read a map." I looked around again. "And if I could read a map...I wouldn't even know where to start."

Kachina took hold of my hands. "Don't worry, Danny. Moon and Stars are excellent sailors; they will get you home safety."

I turned to see that Moon and Stars had already accompanied Lisa and Kim into the *Margaret K* and were now lifting Stephanie and Alexander into the boat as well.

I turned back to Kachina, holding her hands tightly and not wanting to let go. "What about you? Aren't you coming?"

"No, Danny. I must stay here as a watchman over the Stone of Time."

"But I want you to come," I blurted out, embarrassing myself. "I want to hear more stories about Q and the other Travelers," I quickly added, trying to hide the real reason I wanted her to come.

"Danny, I know you will miss me," Kachina said softly. "And I will miss you. But remember"—she paused, placing her hand on my chest, directly over my heart—"We are connected in mind and spirit. I will come to you in your sleep with wondrous stories of Q and the other Travelers, as well as visitors we have had on the island." She let go of my hand so she could wipe the tears from her eyes. "Danny, no matter where you go I will never be more than a thought away."

I grabbed both her hands, again blurting out, "But I don't want to say good-bye."

"Danny, my heart is yours and your heart mine. We will never say good-bye, but we must say farewell." She leaned in close and kissed my check. The entire world felt like it was spinning backward and upside down. I tried to turn and walk away, but I couldn't take my eyes off hers.

I was walking away backward, when suddenly I heard everyone yelling, "Danny, watch out!"

It was too late, I tripped and fell and was now sitting waist deep in water.

I'm not sure if it was the cold water or the loud laughter coming from the boat that brought me back to my senses, but I do remember Moon and Stars hauling me out of the water into the boat.

"Confuzzled?" Kachina looked at Stephanie, both of them trying not to laugh.

"Positively, completely confuzzled," Stephanie answered, and then nodded her head toward Alexander. "Right?" she asked

"Right." Alexander replied

"Don't worry, Danny." Moon slapped me on the back and winked. "I think my sister likes you too."

Sailing away from the beach across the lagoon toward the cave that would take us home, I only had one thought in mind.

I couldn't wait to return to Tiger Island and to Kachina—little did I know how soon that would be.

The End